Lily's Driftwood Bay

The Sunshine Picnic

Let's find sea treasure!

centum

LILY'S DRIFTWOOD BAY: THE SUNSHINE PICNIC

A CENTUM BOOK HB 978-1-910916-70-4 PB 978-1-910916-16-2

Lily's Driftwood Bay™ © Copyright Sixteen South Limited 2015

Lily's Driftwood Bay™ and Driftwood Bay® and logo, characters

and elements are trademarks of Sixteen South Limited.

Published in Great Britain by Centum Books Ltd

Centum Books Ltd, Centum Books, 20 Devon Square,Newton Abbot, Devon,

TQ12 2HR, UK books@centumbooksltd.co.uk

CENTUM BOOKS Limited Reg. No. 07641486

This edition published 2016

A CIP catalogue record for this book is available

from the British Library.

Printed in China

1 3 5 7 9 10 8 6 4 2

Hello! I'm Lily.
I live by the sea with my Dad
and my best friend, Gull.
We live in a beach hut. Inside there's my
telescope that I use to spot sea
treasures that have washed up on the beach.
When Gull and I find sea treasure,
it always starts a fun adventure
across the way on Driftwood Bay!
Are you ready to come with us today?

Helping my Dad with the shopping is always fun because after we have put it all away we choose something tasty to make for dinner!

"What are we having for dinner tonight, Dad?" I ask.
"Hmm.....," Dad thinks.

We both think very hard, but then Gull appears, squawks loudly and points to the beach.

4

"Sea treasure, Dad. I'm going to go and see what it is, Okay?"

"Okay, Lily! I'll be here cooking if you need me!" says Dad, smiling!

5

Down on the beach we find some
sea treasure washed ashore!

"Look Gull! It's a wooden spoon!
But what do you think it's for?

Maybe it's for stirring
a big pot of stew!
Maybe it's for gobbling
a sticky pudding!
Or maybe it's for making
a yummy cake...

across the way on
Driftwood Bay...

6

"All aboard for Driftwood Bay!" comes a voice from the sea.
It's Salty and Delilah, his trusty boat.

"Coming aboard Captain Salty!" I shout.

"Aye, aye, Lily!" says Salty, as he fits my life jacket.

Salty sounds Delilah's horn and off we sail across
the way to Driftwood Bay.

"This might be the sunniest day of the year," says Salty. "Perfect weather for the Driftwood Bay picnic!"

"A picnic! We love a picnic, don't we Gull?" I say. Gull sqwuaks in agreement.

"Nonna's made some delicious Puffin Muffins for me," says Salty. "Maybe she can help you make something for the picnic, too?"

"What a good idea!" I say. "Let's make something really tasty using our sea treasure, Gull,"

We arrive at the Shiphouse Store and we jump off Delilah onto the jetty.

"Thanks Salty! Gull and I are off to make something really yummy!"

"I'll see you at the picnic this afternoon," says Salty.

"What do you think we should make, Gull?" I ask as we walk to Nonna's.

"How about really really wobbly strawberry jelly?"

"Squawk!" – Gull isn't quite sure.

"What about some star shaped cookies?"

"Squawk!" – Gull still isn't quite sure!

"Or how about some banana bread that's gooey and squishy?"

"Squawk!" Gull says to keep thinking.

Gull and I are still thinking what to make as we pass by Wee Rabbit's Treehouse.

"OH NO!" comes a voice.

"That sounds like Wee Rabbit, let's go and see if she is okay, Gull!"

Up in the Treehouse, Wee Rabbit looks upset.

"Oh Lily, can you help?" she asks. "I just can't decide what picnic food to make. It has to be colourful!"

"Hmm..Something colourful ... What about carrot sticks?"

"That's a good idea, Lily!" says Wee Rabbit. "What are you going to bring?"

"I'm not sure yet," I say. "Come on, Gull, let's go and see Nonna!"

On the way, we pass Bull who is looking very excited.

"Hi, Bull!" I shout to him.

"Oh, hi Lily! I'm picking dandelions to make dandelion fizz for the picnic."

"Ooh! That sounds delicious!" Gull squawks loudly!

"Can you help me pick all these dandelions, Lily?" asks Bull. "I need lots of them to make my dandelion fizz taste just right."

As we're helping Bull, we hear the rattling of the Clickety Clackety Train. It's Hatsie!

"Oh, bananas!" says Hatsie, as she stops the train with a screech, making the bananas fall about everywhere!

"What are all these bananas for, Hatsie?" asks Bull.

"To make banana and honey sandwiches for the picnic!" says Hatsie.

"Yum! I can't wait for the picnic!" says Bull heading back towards his paddock. "Thanks Lily!"

"Lily, please could you help me pick up these bananas?" asks Hatsie.

"Of course, Hatsie," I say.

One banana, two bananas, three bananas, four....

Soon we've picked them all up and Gull and I are back on our way to see Nonna.

"I know what we could make, Gull... A cake!"

"Squawk!" - Gull likes this idea!

As we get closer to the Café, we both smell something really, REALLY good.

"It smells like Nonna is already baking a cake!"
I say to Gull.

"Hello, dear," says Nonna.

"Hi, Nonna! Something smells lovely."

"Why thank you, Lily. I'm VERY busy making
a special cake for the picnic."

"Oh dear. Are you too busy to help us
make a cake for the picnic?" I ask.

"I'm afraid I am, Lily dear.
But, this cake has an extra
special recipe. It says that the
icing needs to be mixed by two
people. Will you help me mix it?"

"Yes, Nonna! I'd love to!" I say.
"I even have my own wooden spoon!"

Nonna washes my spoon and I help her mix and mix and mix the icing until it is really soft and creamy.

"Thank you, Lily!" says Nonna after all the mixing is done. "I think this will be my best cake yet, thanks to you!"

At the picnic, everyone has brought something to share. Everyone, that is except Gull and I.

"Welcome, one and all to the most fabulous Driftwood Bay Picnic," says Lord Stag. "Please, tuck in!"

"Squeak, Squeak, Squeak!" the Squeaky Mice say in delight.

"Slipperin' Scallions!" says Salty. "What a wonderful picnic this is!"

"I'm sorry that Gull and I didn't bring anything," I tell everyone.

"You helped me decide
what to bring!"
says Wee Rabbit.

"And you helped me pick
dandelions for my fizz,"
says Bull.

"I couldn't have made my
sandwiches without you,"
says Hatsie.

"And you helped me make
my best cake yet!"
says Nonna.

"Hooray!" we all say.

"Lily...!" calls Dad.

"It's time to go home now."

Back at the beach hut, it's time for dinner!

"I've made your favourite dinner tonight, Lily"

Dad and I tuck in to a big bowl of seafood spaghetti!

It has been a wonderful day of enjoying wonderful food!

Read It Again Activities!

Can you answer these questions now that you have read the story? If you're not sure, then read the story again.

1 Who told Lily about the Driftwood Bay picnic?

2 What did Wee Rabbit bring to the picnic?

3 What ingredient did Bull need for his special fizz?

4 What tool did Nonna use to make her cake icing nice and smooth?

5 Where did they have the picnic?

Lots to Spot!

Check your answers on page 32!

Read the story again, can you find the things below in the pages?

Cup

Post Box

Bowl

Hat

Sandwiches

Beach Ball

Picnic Time!

Have your own Driftwood Bay Picnic! Plan the perfect picnic for you and your friends. Always ask a grown-up's permission and ask for their help in organising!

Where?

A great place to have a picnic is in the garden or at the park. Or under your favourite tree!

Lily's tip:

Even if it's raining outside you can still have your picnic indoors – all you need is a blanket, friends and food!

Who?

Make invites for your friends. Use card or paper, then decorate your invite with doodles of your favourite sea treasures!

You are invited
to Lily's Sunshine Picnic!

Where: The Beach
When: Tomorrow

What: Yummy food and drink!

Hope you can come!

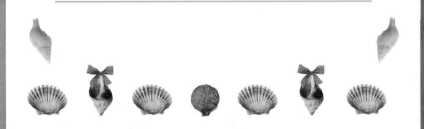

Lily's tip:

Try using recycled or scrap paper, or even cereal box card!

What?

Then it is time to decide what everyone will bring to the picnic. If you all decide to bring something different to share then you'll be sure to have lots of different food and drink to try!

Lily's tip:

If you are stuck on what to bring, then there are lots of other ways you can help your friends – such as organising the cups and plates!

31

Answers!

Read It Again Activities!

1. It was salty!
2. Carrot sticks.
3. Dandelions.
4. A wooden spoon.
5. At the Thinking Tree.

Lots To Spot!

The cup is on page 4.

The hat is on pages 16 and 17.

The post box is on page 18.

The bowl is on page 21.

The sandwiches are on page 25.

The beach ball is on pages 5 and 27.